This Book Belongs To:

While this book is dedicated to all past and present members of my family who have experienced a deep love of West Virginia, it is especially dedicated to my husband, Billy Atkins, who embodies all of the positive character traits presented in this book and thinks that I can do anything.

- Carolyn Peluso Atkins

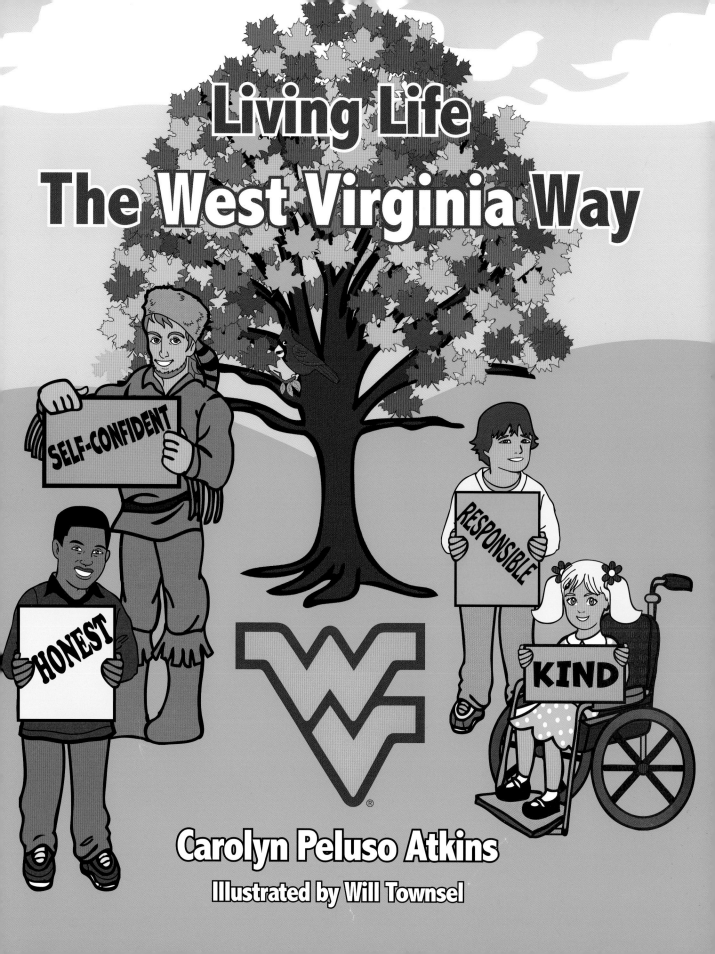

Living Life
The West Virginia Way

SELF-CONFIDENT

HONEST

RESPONSIBLE

KIND

Carolyn Peluso Atkins
Illustrated by Will Townsel

The word "mountaineer" means many things. It means someone who lives in the mountains. Or it means someone who climbs mountains for fun.

It could also be someone who lives in the Appalachian Mountains of West Virginia, the oldest mountain range in the United States.

They are over 250 million years old. They were here before the dinosaurs!

West Virginia used to be part of another state: Virginia. Together, they looked like this. On June 20, 1863, West Virginia left Virginia and became a state of its own. Some people do not know that!

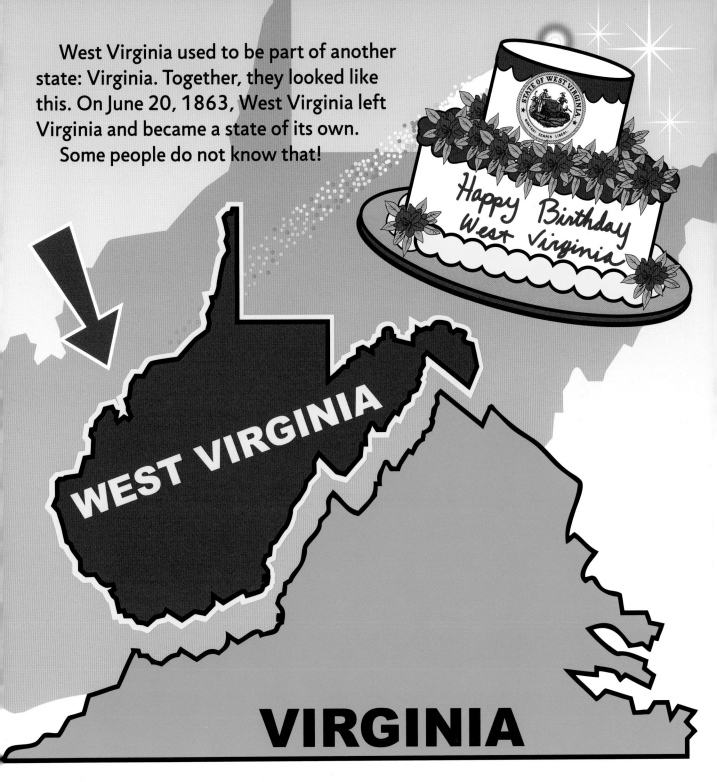

West Virginia Day is on June 20. Happy birthday, West Virginia! West Virginia's nickname is the Mountain State. This makes sense since it is in the Appalachian Mountains!

Do you know anyone with a nickname? Do you have a nickname?

Let's learn about some of the symbols of the state of West Virginia! A symbol is a sign that means something.

The state seal represents either the people who live there or something about the state. West Virginia's seal is a circle. There are two hard-working men on each side of the big rock.

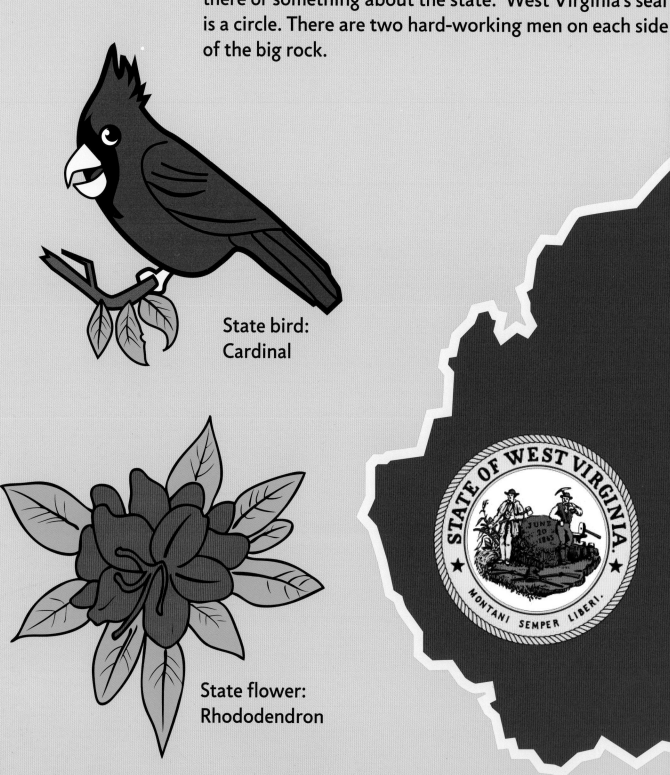

State bird:
Cardinal

State flower:
Rhododendron

The state motto is a group of words that describe a rule or goal to live by. West Virginia's motto is "Mountaineers are always free."

The motto is on the state seal and on the state flag, but it is written in a very old language, Latin: Montani Semper Liberi.

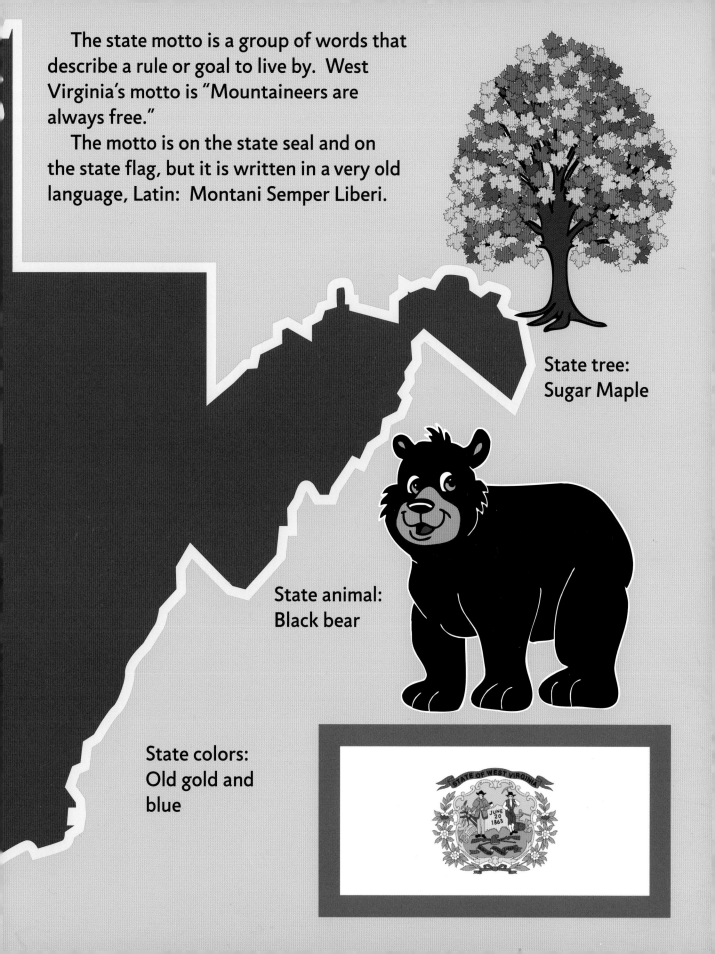

State tree:
Sugar Maple

State animal:
Black bear

State colors:
Old gold and
blue

There are a lot of fun things to do in West Virginia. You can camp outside. You can hike or climb mountains in some of the state parks and forests. You can ride in a boat or raft on the lakes and rivers. You can ski or ice skate.

You can pick your own fresh fruit in the summer and fall. West Virginia's state fruit is the Golden Delicious apple.

You also can attend a university which is a school for students to continue learning after high school. The two largest ones in West Virginia are West Virginia University in Morgantown and Marshall University in Huntington. West Virginia University is also called WVU.

There are lots of fun things to do at a university. You can live with your best friends. You can read all kinds of books and use the computers in the big libraries.

At WVU, you can ride the PRT to class. The PRT is a little car that rides on a rail around campus.

At a university, you can study something that you love to learn about. Is it acting or dancing or singing or drawing?

Is it learning how to make clothes? Is it owning an ice cream store? It is up to you! Start thinking about it now. What do you want to be when you grow up?

Do you want to be a teacher and learn how to teach?
Do you want to be an author and learn how to write books?

Do you want to be an engineer and learn how to build buildings, bridges, and roads?

A logo is a picture that represents something. West Virginia University's logo is called the Flying WV and it looks like this.

The school's colors are Old gold and blue, like the state's colors.

A logo can be on many things: a building, a flag, a cup, or clothing. Can you think of someone who wears a logo?

Athletes are people who play sports like football, basketball, and baseball. Cheerleaders lead cheers for their teams. Fans are people who really like something.

The athletes and cheerleaders wear the logo on their uniforms so people know where they go to school. Fans wear the logo on clothing so people know which team is their favorite.

Do you have clothes with a logo?

A mascot is someone or something that represents a school or a team. It may be a person, animal, or thing. The mascot goes to all the games and cheers for all the sports. The fans love their mascots!

Marshall's mascot is Marco the Buffalo. When buffaloes live together, the group is called a herd. When they run, they make a loud noise like thunder. The Marshall sports teams and fans are called the Thundering Herd.

The Marshall fans clap their hands over their heads when their team scores. It is called the Thunder Clap because it is so loud. At the games, the fans cheer, "Let's go, Herd!" or "We are...Marshall!"

The Marshall fans and players love their band called the Marching Thunder.

WVU's Mountaineer mascot is a person who wears buckskins and carries a musket. Buckskin is soft gold leather that comes from deerskin. A musket is a very large gun. The Mountaineer shoots it into the air when the team scores.

The WVU sports teams and their fans are also called the Mountaineers.

When the Mountaineer Marching Band forms the shape of West Virginia on the football field, the fans clap and cheer, "Let's go, Mountaineers!"

WVU fans are proud of their band too! That is why they nicknamed it The Pride of West Virginia.

If the Mountaineers win, the fans sing a song, *"Country roads...take me home...to the place...I belong...West Virginia...mountain mama...take me home, country roads."*

Do you know that song?

A tradition is something that you have been doing for a long time and will continue to do in the future. Here are some examples of traditions: singing songs after a win, yelling certain cheers, clapping a certain way, and shooting the musket when the team scores.

Do you and your family have traditions? Does your school have traditions? What are they?

Another tradition West Virginians have is trying to do the right thing every day. It does not matter where West Virginians live, where they go to school, which team they cheer for, or whether they are girls or boys. What matters is the way West Virginians live their lives.

What matters is character. What is character? Your character is the REAL YOU!

Character is always doing the right thing, even if nobody is watching you.

Just like Marco the Buffalo represents Marshall University and the Mountaineer represents WVU, there is something that represents all people from West Virginia: good character.

People with good character act like this:

1. They are honest. Telling the truth is one of the most important parts of good character.

2. They are responsible. They keep their promises and they do what they are supposed to do.

3. They believe in themselves. They have self-confidence. They do not try to be like others, but they are happy with themselves.

4. They are kind, caring, and helpful. They are not bullies. Bullies hurt others on purpose. Bullying is teasing, hitting, shoving, or hurting someone. Bullying includes writing, drawing, or saying bad things about someone. People with good character know that bullying is never okay.

5. They respect others. They use the right words and a nice tone of voice when they talk to others. They do not shout. They listen, pay attention, and do not interrupt when others are talking. They answer questions when they are asked.

6. They have courage. They do the right thing even if they are afraid to do it.

7. They are humble. Humble people think about others more than themselves. They do not think they are better than anyone else. If they do something that is good, they do not tell everyone about it. That is called bragging.

8. They work hard. They do their homework and sometimes they do more than they are asked. If the teacher asks them to learn ten words and they learn more than ten, the teacher knows that they are interested and they work hard. Doing more is a good thing. It is very important to be good students!

9. They believe in teamwork. They work well with others, they get along with everyone, and they do their share. They follow rules!

10. They are good sports. That means they are nice whether they win or lose. They do not get angry if others win. Instead, they say this to the winner: "Good game!"

What have you learned about character?

- It is very important.
- It is not something you can buy.
- It is the REAL YOU.
- It is part of you for the rest of your life.
- It is not something that you can pretend.

Do YOU have good character?

Are you honest?
Do you tell the truth?

Are you responsible?
Do you do what you are supposed to do?

Do you believe in yourself?
Do you do what you know is the right thing even if someone tries to get you to do the wrong thing?

Are you caring, kind, and helpful?
Do you care about and help other people?

Do you respect others?
Do you listen, pay attention, answer questions, and use the right words and a nice tone of voice?

Do you have courage?
Do you do the right thing even when you are afraid to do it?

Are you humble?
Do you think about others more than yourself?

Do you work hard?
Do you do more than you have to do in school and at home?

Are you a good team member?
Do you get along with others? Do you follow the rules?

Are you a good sport?
Do you say, "Good job!" when someone else wins?

If your answer is "YES" to all of those questions, then...Congratulations!

You are living life the West Virginia way!

CERTIFICATE AWARDED TO

West Virginia

for

LIVING LIFE THE WEST VIRGINIA WAY

Awarded by _____

KIND

RESPONSIBLE

The End

Professor Carolyn Peluso Atkins grew up in Morgantown, West Virginia, and teaches at West Virginia University. Her husband attended both Marshall University and WVU. Dr. Atkins created Student Athletes Speak Out (SASO), a character education program in 1990. WVU athletes enrolled in her public speaking class have read storybooks and presented speeches to thousands of elementary, middle, and high school students in the Morgantown area. She has also developed and sent DVDs featuring the athletes to all middle schools in West Virginia.

For a list of discussion questions and to download a certificate for living life the West Virginia way, visit **http://saso.wvu.edu**.